Matchbox Mountain

Stories based on a mountain childhood

Amy Ammons Garza

Illustrated by Doreyl Ammons

Bright Mountain Books, Inc.
Asheville, North Carolina

Printed in the United States of America
This book is printed on acid-free paper to insure longevity.

ISBN: 0-914875-24-8

The publisher acknowledges with appreciation permission to
reprint stories which first appeared in the following magazines:
"Matchbox Mountain" — *Appalachian Heritage Magazine*, Berea
College, Berea, KY 40404; "Daddy's Miracle Shoots" —
Transport Fleet News, 1300 W. Exchange Avenue, Chicago, IL
60609; "My Cucumber Doll" — *The Good Old Days*, 306 E. Parr
Road, Berne, IN 46711; "A Twist of a Tale" — *Now and Then*,
Center for Appalachian Studies and Services, East Tennessee
State University, Johnson City, TN 37614; "Willie the
Groundhog" and "A Shoe-Box Christmas" — *Skylark*, Purdue
University, Hammond, IN 46323

Library of Congress Cataloging-in-Publication Data

Garza, Amy.
    Matchbox mountain : stories based on a mountain
childhood / Amy Ammons Garza ; illustrated by Doreyl
Ammons.
        p.   cm.
    ISBN 0-914875-24-8
    1. Garza, Amy–Childhood and Youth. 2. Appalachian
Region, Southern–Social life and customs. 3. Mountain
life–Appalachian Region, Southern. 4. Mountain life–
North Carolina.   I. Ammons, Doreyl, 1943- ill. II. Title.
F217.A65G37 1994
975.04'092–dc20
    [B]   94-36115

Contents

We Three

Daddy worked long and hard without complaint. As a jack-of-all-trades, he performed miracles at anything and everything in order to earn a living for Mother, my younger sister and brother, and me, so we moved around the southern states a great deal in my very young years.

When I was ten years old our family lived in a small house behind a tavern in Augusta, Georgia. Daddy held three jobs at the time. I remember Augusta as the place where Doris, David, and I stayed in trouble. Many were the whippings we received, for our laughter, muffled under bedcovers, still disturbed our father as he struggled to close his eyes for his four hours of sleep.

The day we left Augusta for Tuckasegee, North Carolina, Daddy bought a stake truck, and we loaded everything we owned onto the back of that old International. I guess I tried to help too much, winding up on the receiving end of a lot of pain. As we were loading the washing machine, Daddy accidently dropped it on my finger and just about cut it off. Mother wrapped a rag around it and sat me on a rocking chair in the bed of the truck. And there I sat while Doris and David were allowed to ride next to the cab and feel the wind in their faces.

The air turned cool as we wound our way ever upward into the Appalachian Mountains, while the road twisted and turned like a hairpin. Each time we swerved into a turn, that old chair would rock forward and I would look over the side of the truck—down, down, down the steep edge of Route 107. And with every jolt, I could feel my heart pounding in my aching finger.

Just at twilight we turned off the pavement onto Grassy Creek Road, crossed a narrow bridge that stretched over the Tuckasegee River, and began climbing the last grade we were to climb that day. Darkness closed around us as Daddy edged the tipsy truck down a road cut deep into the side of a mountain toward a rickety old house hidden in the valley below.

I still can see the red tar paper that wrapped around the sinister-looking house in which we were to live for the next three years. There was no electricity, no plumbing, no neighbors, no way to go anywhere but walk, no kids to play with, no television, no stores near by. There was nothing but mountains and trees! But, it was here we three created our own special childhood memories—memories of matchbox cars and lollipop pigs, cucumber dolls, "prayer meetings" in the old canhouse, "dipping snuff" made of cocoa and water, making "snowcream" in the winter and clover chains in the spring; memories of dropping seeds into earth cool between our bare toes, watching baby groundhogs tumble and play, picking blackberries in the wilds of a thicket, leaning over a log to come face to face with a water moccasin, and discovering the one and only Santa Claus.

Well, all of Daddy's work finally bore fruit; we three did grow up. David became a teacher, Doris an artist, and I an author—all professions that require creativity.

We live miles apart, but every so often, we gather at Grassy Creek, walk that same road together, retell and relive those years in our special hollow in the Carolina mountains. It all began the year I was ten, Doris nine, and David seven . . . the year we moved away from Augusta and came home to mystical, magical Tuckasegee Valley.

The stories that follow are gifts from the three of us—the Ammons kids.

Matchbox Mountain

Surrounded by mountains, the only sounds that of many birds singing, creeks rushing, and wind blowing, we three began our life there at Grassy Creek as children of the earth. With wide eyes we leapt into the newness with anticipation.

In the mountain bank close to our house, Doris, David, and I built a little make-believe city. It shone with sophistication and ingenuity. We made buildings from old tomato soup cans; we fashioned homes from eggshells; we turned fruit jars upside down to represent water towers. We even put up filling stations where straight wooden clothespins served as gas pumps. The road system we constructed would wind all around the bank, up and down, and beneath the overhang of the graveled road above our house. And since we had no "store-bought" toy cars, we manufactured our own cars and trucks from matchboxes and small aspirin bottles.

I hauled all kinds of loads in my matchbox dump truck—my logs were mostly broken sticks—unloading them at my brother's "sawmill," on the other side of the bank. There were times when I would wreck my dump truck and have to watch it float down the nearby creek. From "passion plants" that grew alongside Grassy Creek Road, we collected all of its fruit we could find (which we called "lollipops") and made all sizes of pigs for our hog pens. The legs were made of tiny sticks, and curly red tendrils from wild grapevines made colorful tails. David developed quite good imitations of pig grunts and squeals, even to throwing in a few good mud rolls every once in a while.

Doris spent more time drawing in the dirt than driving her matchbox car. She loved the birds she had seen Grandpa whittle, so she drew them in all kinds of shapes and movements. Then, she'd sit for hours above us, watching the bluebirds dart down, the hummingbirds hang in space as they drew from the nectar of the passion flowers, and the cardinals that seemed to command attention by filling the limbs of the giant oak towering over our home. Sometimes I still wake at night and hear Doris's cry, "Look, there's another cardinal . . . make a wish! It'll come true!"

David milked all our play cattle, hauling the milk to my general store at the crossroads of Matchbox Mountain. I made good leaf money selling all my goods: brooms made from twigs of a bush tied together, more matchbox trucks, rocks for rock houses, clothespins, June bugs with strings tied around them, buttons (for dishes), and miscellaneous odds and ends.

What a time we had bartering and trading, fussing and laughing, putting our lips together and making the

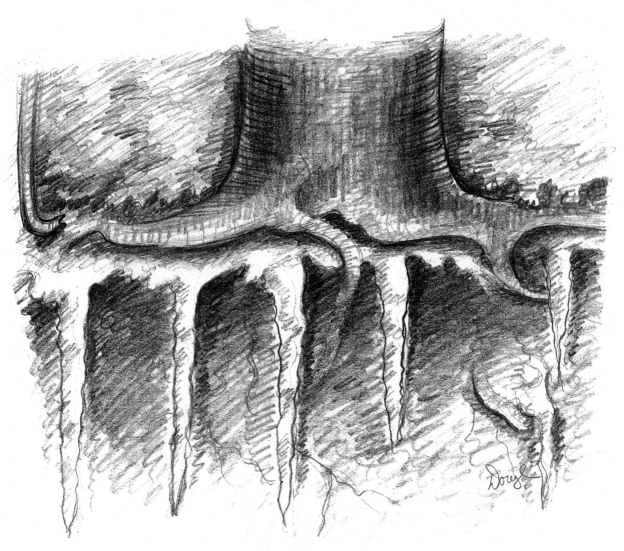

uuudin, uuudin noise of many trucks as they traveled our play roads.

In the months to come the little city was never washed away by rain; it was sheltered by the overhang of the bank. Only in winter did it disappear, for icicles formed on the brim of the bank and sometimes tore the complete overhang apart. But, as time went on, the seasons would change, bringing dryness to the earth underneath the overhang below Grassy Creek Road, and once again construction would begin on Matchbox Mountain—our mountain of creativity.

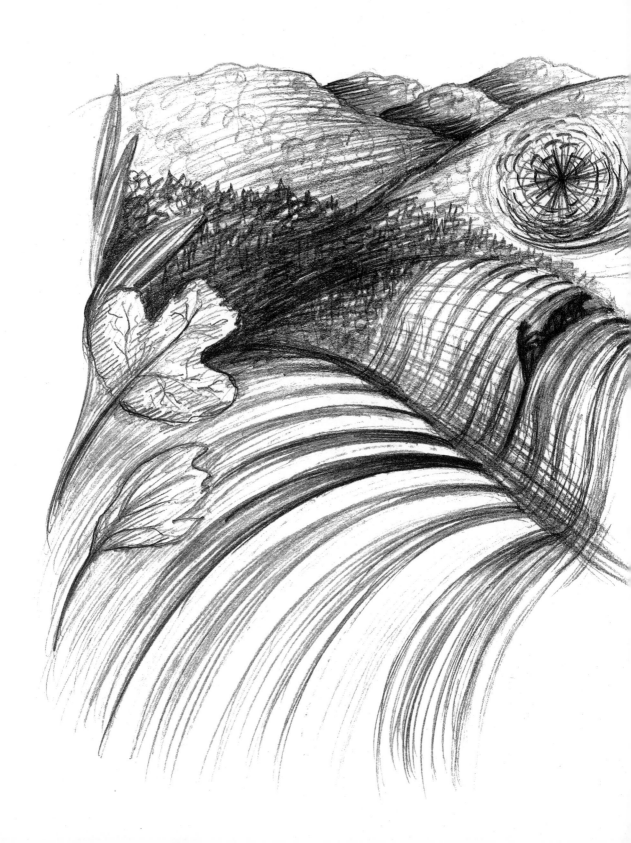

Daddy's Miracle Shoots

When cottonwood puffs go flying through the air, I remember springtime in the mountains, and miracle shoots. Springtime brought planting time, and planting time brought miracles.

Following along behind Daddy as he plowed fall's stubble, the reins of old Dan draped over his shoulders, I would dig my bare feet in freshly turned earth, hopping along to the tune of "gee, haw—gee, haw!"

The garden Daddy laid out wasn't like the ones I've seen in magazines, flat with rows neatly spaced as far as the eye can see. Our garden followed the slope of the land as it dipped and rolled over and around the mountainside. Sometimes I could still hear Daddy directing the horse, but I couldn't see him. Nearby, I could hear the soothing swish of the wind in the treetops and feel its passage in the billow of my skirt against my knees. The presence of the warm sun on my back; the warble of bobwhites, thrushes, and cardinals; the gurgle of the creek below—all these feelings and sounds—kept me company.

Long rows would lap around the hill, the plowed ground cool and slightly damp, leaving behind squirming worms and tiny snails. I inspected them closely, holding them carefully in the palms of my hands. At times I would be so engrossed I'd have to run to get out of the way of old Dan as he would come suddenly and powerfully over the rise for another turn around the mountain.

Then, what a thrill I'd get when Daddy would entrust me with the seeds destined to be our food for the year. Dropping the yellow corn, two in a hill a foot apart, brought me even closer to the earth. Then patting them in safely would bring me even closer yet to the peaceful, tender soil.

When Daddy would stop to water and rest old Dan, he would take time to sit under the huge arms of an oak and call me to him. What discussions we had then! "Daddy, where does corn come from?" I'd ask.

Daddy would chew on a blade of grass, squint his eyes at the sun, then hug me closely and say, "That's not corn, Amy; it's a small piece of a big miracle."

"But, Daddy, how can that be?"

"You know a miracle is something marvelous that happens no one can truly explain, like springtime, or flowers, or like corn. You can see how hard the corn kernel is, can't you? Well, when it goes into the soil, this hard seed suddenly is hidden from all human eyes. There, in the dark, it slowly softens and suddenly out bursts a new growth—a tiny corn stalk."

"But, Daddy, I've dug up a corn seed just to see what

10

happens, and it has a long white hard string on it that's turned upside down. It looks all ugly then."

"That string is the corn's root, Amy," Daddy would say, smiling wide. "The root slides deep in the ground, while the tiny stalk shoots its way up to the surface. That's why those small green stalks are called 'corn shoots' when they first come up."

"Are corn shoots miracles, too?"

"Yes, they are. 'Cause without the corn seed there would be no corn shoots." Daddy would hold me closer. "You, and your sister and brother, are my miracle seeds—my corn shoots!" Then Daddy would stand, and placing his hand on my head, he'd continue, "See how you're shooting up!"

I would laugh and run around him. "I'm going to get real tall someday, Daddy. Just you wait and see!"

"Well, time to get back to creating miracles!" And with those words, he'd hand me my sack of corn seed, and say as he draped the reins about his neck, "Don't forget now, remember to be caring about the seed. Give it a good hill to grow in and soon we'll have miracle shoots popping up all over the place!" Then, he'd move off, calling, "Come on, Dan, gee up, gee, haw."

"But, Daddy, you never told me where corn really came from in the first place!" I would call, watching his back jerk with the strain of the plow digging through the ground.

But the special time with Daddy would be gone then. He was a hard-working man, given to spending more time trying to make a living for his family than spending time talking. Now every year when I see cottonwood puffs go flying through the air, I remember springtime in the mountains and that I was one of Daddy's miracle shoots.

Willie the Groundhog

Behind a large moss-covered rock at the edge of the forest, we lay in hiding. In the pasture below, partially covered by an old rotten stump, was a gaping black hole. There was the sound of rushing water from the nearby Grassy Creek, and the call of a bobwhite in the distance. Beside me, David pressed himself closer to the rock, frozen in silence. Only his eyes moved as he strained to catch any movement near the dark hole.

I leaned closer to my brother, putting a finger to my lips. "Sh-h-h," I whispered, "don't make a sound. Willie will be out soon, just you wait and see!" David gave me his best don't-you-see-I'm-not-talking disgusted look and then turned his gaze back to the entrance of the groundhog den.

I smiled. Willie and I were friends. I had been spying on him for almost two months now. There had been days when I had sat for hours and hadn't seen hide nor hair of him. Then, sometimes on sunny days I had watched him a big part of a morning. On these days, I felt that he had watched me as much as I had watched him. Thus this friendship had blossomed, enough so that today I was hoping Willie would venture forth into the sunlight and allow my brother to see his first live groundhog.

The cool spring morning had vanished. In its place was the heat of the noonday sun. The rays blazed down on our heads as the sun climbed higher into the

13

heavens. Against the blue sky, white puffy clouds hovered near the horizon, above the green trees. A breeze softly slid around us, bringing with it the sweet smell of honeysuckle. Life seemed to stand still as we waited and watched.

Then there was a swift movement near the mouth of the hole. David grabbed my arm and his eyes widened. I clamped my lips and motioned for David to keep still; our gazes were then fixed on the hole.

Suddenly, there he sat! He seemed to rear back on his haunches to quickly scan the area. His proud features bespoke his authority: this was his kingdom; everything he surveyed was his and his alone!

From our position, we could see well. His head, broad and flat, darted back and forth showing quick flashing eyes and a small black nose. A coarse gray coat covered the upper part of his body, while the belly fur bore a soft yellowish-orange color. Including his bushy tail, he looked to be about two feet long.

As Willie sat there, my gaze fastened on his sharp claws. He held them close to his body as he continued to listen and watch for danger. I had seen those claws dig his burrow and widen the entrance while he scraped the dirt out with his hind feet. Slowly, then, Willie dropped to all four feet and, with a shake of his fur, moved off toward the creek, stopping to eat clover on the way.

"Gosh," David whispered, "ain't he somethin'!" I squeezed his shoulder and nodded.

Willie waded into the creek and stuck his nose in. Just as quickly, he wobbled out, shaking water all about in a fine spray. Back he came toward the burrow. Passing it up, he crawled upon the flat rock

alongside the hole and lay down in the sun, his nose on his paws. His little nose twitched! Willie had the look of total contentment.

David and I grinned at each other. Then David placed his hands on the rock that separated us from Willie, put his chin on top of his hands, and tried to twitch his nose, too! He looked so funny! His nose had been broken a few years back, and it definitely was not the twitching kind.

I almost burst out laughing. Quickly, however, I covered my mouth and just barely saved the giggle that would have spoiled our fun. "David!" I whispered as I gained my composure. David grinned at me as we leaned against the rock to gaze at Willie.

It wasn't long until Willie stirred, raising his head to survey his kingdom again. He seemed to be pleased. Then slowly he sat up, shook his fur, and ambled back toward his den. I was prepared to accept the fact that we'd seen all of Willie we were going to see that day. But just then there was another movement by the entrance of the burrow.

"Oh, Amy! Look at that!" David's voice crept out in awe. Out of the dark of the hole came the smallest groundhog I'd ever seen. And then another . . . and another . . . and another . . . until there were six little groundhogs!

Words were forgotten as we watched Willie. *She* pridefully lay on the grass below us, the three of us mesmerized by a group of scampering balls of fur, rolling and playing in total abandonment. All too soon, Willie decided enough was enough, and giving the little ones a small push with her nose, she herded them away out of sight.

16

"I'll never forget this day, Amy!" David's voice had reverence.

"We'll come back to see them again, David, but not too often. We don't want to scare them," I said, knowing all the time I was wasting my words.

Suddenly, there was Willie again! Sitting on her haunches, staring directly at us, she sat very still and straight. Then she was gone. I think Willie was just letting us know that our presence was known and that it was okay.

For days afterward, urged on by David, we returned to the burrow, watching and waiting, each time disappointed. The brush began to grow over the hole and the grass in the glen grew high. Finally, we gave up. Willie and her brood became a memory.

Then one day, a few months later, as I was returning from weeding our garden, I passed the trail that led to the den. Something seemed to pull me up the shadowed, overgrown path. I found the rock and leaned against it. Below gaped the hole, and there, on the flat rock above it, was Willie! Sitting up tall, she gazed straight at me. We eyed each other, and then after a smile, we each turned to go our own way. You see, we were friends, Willie and I.

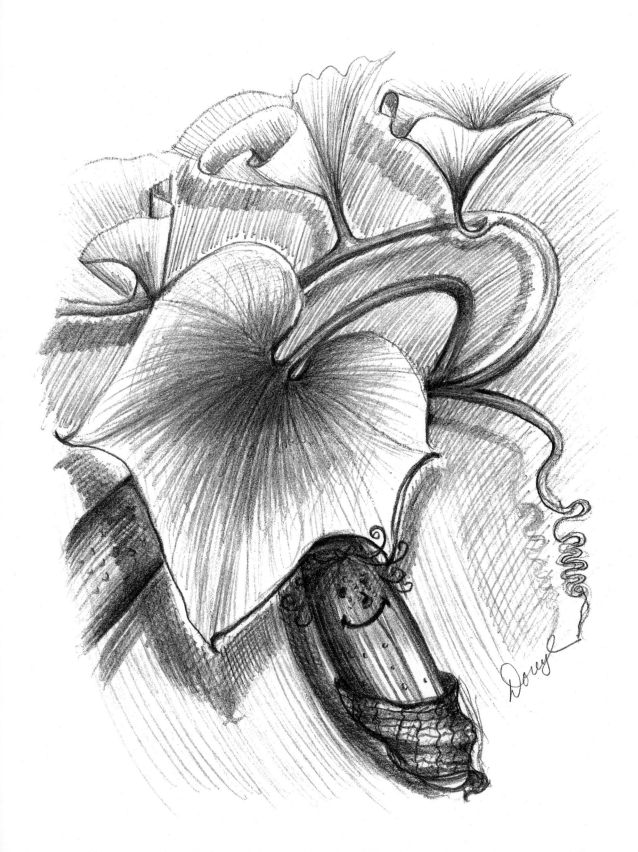

My Cucumber Doll

One of the fondest memories I have of growing up in the Blue Ridge Mountains is of my cucumber doll. When Daddy's cucumbers grew too big for us to eat raw or for Mother to pickle, he gave me permission to "gather" my own "baby."

Far back in the patch, hidden under huge green leaves, I would find her. She would be big, fat, yellow, and a little dirty from the way rain pattered on her, but still firm. With a piece of charcoal I created her eyes, her nose, and her mouth; she always had a smile on her face. Most of the time I didn't worry about her bald head, but sometimes I collected little curly red tendrils from wild grapevines and tied them about her head with a string.

For days I carried her, wrapped in a piece of discarded blanket, until she became too soft to hold. It was with tenderness that I would lay her carefully back in under the leaves and then choose another, firmer cucumber doll.

No matter where I would go, my constant companion would be my cucumber doll. We followed the worn path up the mountain to Grandma Retter's house, singing all the hymns I knew—me in a broken alto voice and my cucumber doll doing nothing but smiling all the while. We'd slide down Grassy Creek Falls, gliding through spring-cold water, screaming. (I'm sure I was the loudest!) We'd sneak through Uncle Bryson's barbed wire fence to get to the big apple tree that grew in the middle of the pasture, all the while keeping an eye open for the mean old bull whose main purpose in life was to guard that tree. We'd hoe rows and rows of tall swaying corn, dreaming of faraway places, yet not being able to see even above the tassels of the corn. Funny, only I would be tired by the end of the day.

I played with my cucumber dolls all during Indian summer, but on the morning of the first heavy frost, I knew the one I was carrying would soon be gone and there would be no more replacements until the following year. During that last week, she became all the more dear, and it was with deep sadness that I laid her beside her sisters. Somehow I knew that for me, the time of the cucumber dolls would soon be over for good.

My cucumber doll was a child of the land, just as I was a child of the land. Even as a youngster, carrying my doll around with me, I knew the land, my Appalachian home, was special. And in my heart I carried, as lovingly as I carried the cucumber doll, an abiding love and pride for my heritage.

"Fraidy-cat"

Close to the side of the mountain behind our home stood a small two-room building. It had one room on the bottom with one room overtop and had been built to store canned goods. Inside, on the ground floor, were shelves going up almost to the ceiling filled with Mother's jars of canned corn, green beans, peas, beets, greens, pickled cucumbers, jams, and jellies. (Hidden behind these were quart jars of Daddy's home-brewed whiskey.) Outside on the black tar-papered boards of the building hung drying skins of rabbits, squirrels, foxes, groundhogs, and once in a while, a bear. The tin roof of the "canhouse," as we called it, had rusted a deep brown.

The small room built above the storage room had once been a tiny bedroom for visitors, I suppose, for it still held a rickety old table with a rusted wash basin and a couple of chairs. And even though we had to climb a ladder affixed to the boards on the back of the canhouse to achieve entrance, Doris, David, and I loved that room. On many wintry days, that was where we held our "revival services" or our "prayer meetings."

On the table in the upper room we had stored the material we needed for our preaching services: an old Bible Uncle Bryson had given us and pages from the Sears and Roebuck catalog which we used for song books. We had the room arranged just right for our service, with the table in the middle of the room and

the chairs in front of it. Each service we held grew to be the same. David would preach at his pulpit while Doris and I would be his singing congregation.

"If you don't quit your wicked ways, you're goin' straight to hell! It's awful hot down there! It ain't no place to be!" David would yell, slinging his arms just the way he'd seen Uncle Bryson do when the older man would get wound up.

"Amen! Amen!" Doris and I would respond.

"Now, get your songbooks, and turn to page ten. Let's all sing 'Shall We Gather at the River.'"

We'd pick up our catalog sheets and begin to sing as loudly as we could. Through the cracked window behind David many times I'd see Daddy stop in his chores to stare at the canhouse when we were holding services. After a while he'd turn and walk away shaking his head.

These upper room services were mostly simple fun, but there was one meeting when our fun turned into cold fear.

The day it happened, Daddy had thrown a bag of corn he had been storing in the canhouse over his shoulder and set off up the mountain toward Grandpa's cabin. Mother had been feeling poorly, so she had confined herself to her bedroom. The overcast day had seemed to put a spell on my brother and me. We had climbed to the top of all the trees we could around the house; we had forded the creek three or four times, hopping on stones to get across and back again; we had swung so high on the old tire Daddy had fastened to the big oak in the front yard that the motion had jerked the rest of the leaves off the tree. When we could think of nothing else to do, we came up with the idea of a game called "walking the plank." We would push a plank Daddy had left at the top of the hill behind the canhouse through the doorway of the upper room and walk across.

We found a piece of rope and then ran to the path that wound its way up the side of the bank, calling for Doris to come join us. She had been busy occupying herself away from all our dare-deviltry. Almost reluctantly, she followed us up the path.

At the top, David and I tugged on the plank, then dragged and pushed until we had it in line with the door. It was surprisingly light. I tied the rope around the plank, then told David to toss one end to me when I got inside the upper room. Then I ran down the path and climbed the ladder. In no time we had the plank in place.

Immediately, David began walking the plank with his arms extended, playfully swinging them back and forth. I climbed down the ladder, and hurried to take my turn, mimicking his actions, hardly noticing the great distance to the ground below. Doris stood to one side, not moving, just watching with big eyes.

"Come on, Doris, walk the plank," I called from the doorway. She didn't budge.

"Doris, come on!" David had started back across. He held out his hand to her. "Come on, I'll help you."

Doris retreated, her hands behind her back, and shook her head.

"You can do it, Doris. Walk the plank! See, I did it." I started across, then stopped and came back.

"NO!" she finally said, loudly.

"Why not? Are you scared?" David now stood with

his hands on his hips, one foot on the plank and one foot on the ground.

"N-n-no."

"Yes, you are! You're a fraidy-cat!" David turned to look at me. "Doris is a fraidy-cat!"

"I am not!" Doris's voice seemed hollow. "Amy, make David stop callin' me that awful name!"

"Fraidy-cat, fraidy-cat, Doris is a fraidy-cat," David sang, twisting his body to the tune. It was my turn to say nothing. I simply stared at Doris.

"Amy!" she cried, "make him quit!"

"Fraidy-cat, fraidy-cat, Doris is a fraidy-cat!" David sang on. I still said nothing. It seemed like hours passed in those few minutes while Doris took in David's badgering and my lack of help.

"All right," she finally said. "I'll . . . walk the plank." Her voice ended in almost a whisper. David ran across the plank to stand beside me, grinning in triumph.

When Doris put her foot on the plank, I could see the trembling of her legs. A warning in my head sounded. Since Mother and Daddy weren't there, maybe it was up to me to stop her if she was afraid. But I hesitated. Instead, I strained to look closely at her face. Tears wet her cheeks. Then, my heart began to pound in my breast, and I opened my mouth. Doris took another step and stood on the plank, her whole body shaking.

"Doris . . . " I began, but she teetered and I couldn't get the words out. Now it seemed that even the plank shook as Doris righted herself and then slowly dragged one foot in front of the other and looked down. She swayed.

"Don't look down!" I finally got out in a raspy cry.

"I'm scar-r-red!" Doris barely got out. "I can't turn!"

"Stay still," I called around the lump that had grown in my throat. "I'll come out to help you."

"NO! It might break! I'll . . . do . . . it!"

A cold hand went in mine, and I glanced down to see tears slide out of the corners of David's eyes. Then Doris wrinkled her forehead, fixed her eyes on me, held her arms out to her sides and slowly teetered toward David and me, one slow staggering step at a time.

And then, something strange began to happen. A soft wind started to blow, gently drying Doris's face. Her back straightened, her head went up, her arms and legs steadied. A new expression crept over her face. This only heightened my fear. It was all I could do to stand still and not scream.

When her fingertips finally touched mine, I grabbed
her with all my power and pulled her off the plank.
The three of us stood there for a long time, our arms
intermingled and wrapped tightly around each other.

"Doris," muttered David from underneath all the
arms, "I take it back; you ain't no fraidy-cat."

We began to laugh; in fact, we laughed until we all
cried. And then quietly, through my tears, I said, "I
think we ought to thank the Lord for watching out for
all of us."

Wiping at our eyes, we turned and started for the
pulpit; then Doris stopped and gazed first at David and
then at me.

"I get to choose the hymn this time," she said with
an impish grin. "I want to sing 'I'll Fly Away'!"

So we did. After we could get our breath.

The Hole in the Wall

The bedroom my sister, brother, and I shared with our parents could not be called *my* bedroom; it was *our* bedroom. So, having my very own hole in the wall of that bedroom was really a big deal. That wonderful hole in the plaster contained a jar with a string tied around the cap and fastened to a nail above the hole.

In that jar was everything I had treasured throughout my ten years. No one knew of my hiding place. I had hidden all evidence well: the string was the color of the wall and a calendar hung from the nail, hiding the string.

Hidden in the jar was a fine writing pen given to me by an older lady with whom I had stayed once, brightly colored buttons taken from a dress the missionary at Tuckasegee had given me, Indian arrowheads I had found on Grassy Creek Road, the biggest buckeye I had ever seen, and cucumber seeds saved from my last cucumber doll—all irreplaceable treasures!

Almost every morning I would lie in bed and dream of my hidden treasures, gazing at the calendar that hid my secrets. Then, one morning something extraordinary happened. I saw the string move the calendar from side to side! I could not believe my eyes. I bounded off the bed, being careful not to wake my sister and brother who slept with me, and rushed over to the hole. I was only a few inches taller than the hole, so I could see inside the plaster very easily.

Removing the calendar, I carefully began to pull on the string. It seemed to be caught on something. More curious than anything else, I leaned closer until my head was almost inside the dark hole in the wall. Just as my eyes began to become adjusted to the blackness, I saw what was making the jar move. It was a blacksnake! It had wrapped itself around the jar and was staring at me, its shiny skin flashing blue silver.

That morning I reacted so differently from the way I normally would, for even though I was deathly afraid of snakes, I wasn't frightened. The blacksnake had found my treasures, but he could not get at them, no matter how he tried. He had found my hiding place; yet, maybe I had found his home.

It was then I decided that we all needed a homeplace and I could share mine. I'd not tell a soul. I knew Mother would scream and Daddy would smoke him out. All that spring and well into the summer, I watched my string move and realized a kind of satisfaction, a secret shared with only a snake.

He must have known he had a friend, for when the blacksnake moved out that fall, he left his skin behind, and I had a new treasure to put in my jar.

Grandpa, Tell Us a Story

High on the mountain above our home, far away from the closest neighbor, Grandpa sat in the old family cabin by the fireplace whittling little birds from oak wood. In the dim light of the kerosene lamp, his frail form cast shadows on the wall. The wind of an approaching storm rattled the tin roof, and then from somewhere outside came the cry of a panther.

As we sat on the floor at his feet, Doris, David, and I shivered and drew closer together. The glowing fire in the fireplace popped and crackled, its blue flames leaping and dancing around the rough-cut logs.

Grandpa's chair creaked as he leaned forward, his piercing eyes shining out of the shadows of his brows. His voice, low and full, seemed to crawl out into the stillness of the room. "Hear that panther squall, way out yonder on the ridge? He's hunting, that panther, hunting them night critters—creeping up on his prey, soft and gentlelike. But them black cats are strong! They can kill a deer on the run, then tote its carcass up a tree. I've seen fellers that's been sliced up by a panther's claws . . . cut bad! And what them claws don't get, them teeth do."

Grandpa, observing our widened eyes, nodded his satisfaction and settled back in his chair. Laying his whittling in his lap, he asked, "Want to hear the tale about when your Grandma Retter came face to face with a fearsome panther on the verge of starvation?"

"Oh, yes, Grandpa, tell us the story!" we cried together, and then we listened to his every word, spellbound.

Retter had been cooking for the men at my lumber camp. It was a far piece over to that neck of the woods, about five miles or so, five miles of rough going straight by the old Larson trail. Since there wasn't anybody to leave the young-uns with, Retter'd been taking the boys with her. Let's see, she had Bryson and Jim, and Albert—he was just a baby.

For every one of them five miles over to Larson Lumber Camp, your grandma used to carry one boy on her hip while the other two hung onto her dress. The four of them walked to the camp early every morning and came home after the dinner dishes were done.

Well, unbeknownst to me, Retter'd been having feelings that something had been following her and the boys on those five-mile treks. That's why she had the knife in her pocket when this thing happened.

Retter and the boys were on their way home. The day had turned off dark and cold and a snowstorm had just started. For some reason on that day I watched them from the porch until the woods closed around them. They looked so little and the storm was getting worse. I told my crew to quit, clean up, and call it a day. I wanted to try and catch Retter and the boys before they got too far.

With the snow swirling all around, Retter could hardly see. She told me later she knew as soon as she got into the woods that there was something wrong; she could feel eyes watching her, eyes that filled her skin with goose quills.

Trying not to let the boys know how uneasy she was, she walked fast. Above her, on the rocky ledge that ran alongside the trail, she could hear, real quiet, the rustle of something walking in the dead leaves. She stopped, straining to hear. There wasn't nothing. She started again; the pat . . . pat . . . pat above her started again, too. She stopped; it stopped. She started; it started. Shivers crawled up her backside.

Retter knew something was there—she could almost feel the breathing of it—but she fought against getting so scared she couldn't take care of the boys. She walked faster. The falling snow had lighted the trail in front of her, but in the darkness of the woods pushing close, it seemed all kinds of shapes were standing there, leaning close, watching her.

Bryson and Jim began whimpering; Albert was weighing heavy on her aching side. Then all of a sudden, Retter realized she couldn't hear the footsteps on the ledge anymore. That worried her more than anything else. She stopped, caught her breath, and listened real careful, wondering. Just ahead of her was a turn in the trail; she knew there was a big oak just around that bend. She put her hand on the knife she had in her apron pocket, thinking for a minute that she should send the boys back toward the camp, then changed her mind. She wasn't letting them boys out of her sight!

Something told Retter there was danger just around that corner. The back of her neck stiffened; she drew Albert closer. Her fingers in her apron pocket curled strong around the knife handle. She moved forward, turning the bend.

Just in the middle of that bend was the big oak with a long, heavy limb hanging out over the trail. Retter let her eyes travel up the darkness of the trunk, out onto that naked limb, to the sudden shiny-red eyes of a panther! He was crouched into a ball of blackness on that limb.

For a minute, that panther and Retter stared at each other through the flying snowflakes. Then, the panther's jaw quivered and he pulled back his lips, the sudden gleam of his white teeth warning Retter what he was going to do.

Retter tightened her hold on Albert, pulling that baby close to her, swinging her body around to protect him. She yelled to the boys to run back and fetch their pa. The hand that held the knife flew out of her pocket.

That ball of black power leaped and leaped high! He never seen the flash of the knife Retter held up in her steady hand. The arc of him came down full on your grandma, his powerful heart slapping hard on the knife.

When I came running around the bend, followed by Bryson and Jim, I saw that black panther laying overtop your grandma and the baby in the snow. The panther moved! I yelled loud. A blackness came over me like the whip of a knife, but I shook it off. The three of them seemed to be struggling in all that bloody snow. Then I seen it was just Retter trying to push the dead cat off her and Albert. He must have been powerful hungry, for panthers don't normally attack humans lest they're starving.

Well, I got to Retter and Albert and helped pull the

animal to one side. My heart hurt with the fear of what might have happened.

Young-uns, your grandma is special. Don't you ever forget it! I'll always remember her raising up, her arm still around that baby, both of them covered up in blood. All she said was, "We best be getting on home; these young-uns are all tired out."

We'll always remember, Grandpa.

A Twist of a Tale

The forest was cool. The morning sun had yet to feel its way through the dense foliage. Shivering, I hugged my arms tighter as I climbed through the mist. I was on my way to see Aunt Belle. She lived alone at the top of the mountain. Faintly, I could see the trail before me winding its way up the steep incline. For some reason, apprehension began to steal through me, but all I observed were the tall pines and the laurel bushes that pushed their boughs into my path.

Shaking my head, I forced a small laugh from my lips as I thought of the many times I had safely climbed this same trail. What was I suddenly afraid would be here to interrupt my journey? I knew that somewhere ahead the ground would level off and I could pause for a moment and rest.

My breath came in short jerks, joining the damp mist and spreading out like a skinny ghostly finger stealing its way upward. Already there was an ache in my side, and the higher I climbed, the faster the pain traveled, going deep within my side and settling around my heart. As my throat grew raspy and dry, I knew I would have to rest soon.

Then I heard it: the dim sound of rushing water in the distance. Relieved, I realized I had reached the halfway point in my journey. The resting spot was just a bit farther; I pushed myself to climb the short distance to level ground.

Once there, I thankfully stretched and breathed deeply, letting my gaze travel around the small clearing. The restfulness of the scene soothed and relaxed me. Brown pine needles covered the soft earth; bright green leaf-hands reached out to greet me.

The talking waters of the swiftly flowing creek called to me, and I advanced to one of nature's bridges—an old log that had fallen across the creek. Kneeling on the log, I could see through the clear spring water to the sandy creek bottom below. Here the water was deeper and seemed to have its own resting place before continuing its rush downward to discover new worlds.

A sudden movement disturbed the tranquility of the resting water. Brandishing his sword of defense, a crawdad flung himself out to meet a challenger, one of his own kind. A tarnished-black suit of armor covered each of the warriors. Sand flew as each fighter advanced and then circled the other, both using their tails to propel their bodies. Their two front legs were shaped into sharp claws with which they fought gallantly.

Slowly the battle took them underneath the log on which I was kneeling. My interested gaze followed the skirmish, and my body followed my eyes until I found myself leaning way over and looking beneath the log.

Suddenly, I came face to face with a water moccasin! For an eternity, it seemed, we eyed one another.

"S-s-so, my child, have you never s-s-seen a s-s-snake before?"

My eyes felt as if they were going to leap out of their sockets into the water. This snake had spoken to me! I wanted to move, but the strength had fled my legs.

"S-s-speak, dear child. S-s-speak to me."

The crawdads were forgotten; my surroundings were forgotten. The sparkle and glitter of the water moccasin's eyes held me as if I were hypnotized.

"S-s-show me you can s-s-speak, s-s-sweet child. Tell me, has s-s-something got your tongue?" softly hissed the snake. His mouth seemed to turn up at the edges, almost as if he were laughing at me. His tongue darted in and out as he waited for me to speak.

"I don't believe it," I whispered. "Snakes can't talk!"

"S-s-say you don't believe I'm s-s-speaking? S-s-should I move closer?" asked the dark, green-skinned snake, turning so I could see the almost perfect brown circles that banded his body.

"No! Please! Stay where you are," I cried with alarm. "I believe; I can hear your voice!"

"S-s-so right you are, my dear. Tell me, for what

reason do you cros-s-s my log s-s-so s-s-seldom now? My curiosity has the better of me."

"W-what . . . do you m-mean?" I stammered.

"S-s-some time ago your s-s-steps cros-s-sed my log more often, now s-s-so s-s-seldom."

"Well, I guess I don't go see Aunt Belle as often as I used to. She tells the same old stories over and over again. I guess I just get . . . bored," I answered, wondering why I was talking to a snake.

"You no longer love her, child?"

"Of course I love her! I've always loved her. I help her, too. And Aunt Belle is going to help me put together a quilt soon; it's to be mine someday when I marry."

"S-s-such a touching thought . . . tut, tut. Well, my lovely, your days with your Aunt Belle will s-s-soon be over. S-s-she's s-s-soon to be no more, . . . s-s-so s-s-sorry to s-s-say, child."

My heart almost stopped! Did I understand him to say my Aunt Belle was going to die? "No! No! I don't believe it," I cried.

"Why would that make you s-s-so unhappy, child? S-s-she does bore you . . . or s-s-so you s-s-say."

"No! I love her!" I shouted as I jumped up. "I'll go see her!" I was running as I spoke, urgency pushing me up the path.

Behind me, the snake called, "S-s-slow down, child, or you will s-s-slide and fall. S-s-s-o-o long!"

Just as I heard the last hissing sound from the snake, I stumbled and began to fall. I felt as if I were falling into deep darkness; I felt myself scream. The next thing I knew, hands were on me, shaking hard.

"Amy, Amy! Wake up! You've had a nightmare." As I opened my eyes, my mother's face loomed above me, concern written in the lines of her forehead.

"It's okay, Mother. I'm awake now." I raised myself and rubbed my eyes. The sun's morning light streamed into the bedroom. My dream had been so real, I was still looking for the snake.

Aunt Belle! Suddenly, I knew she must need me. I dressed and sped out of the house faster than I had ever before. The trail up the mountain was damp with dew still on the ground and the leaves of the trees. When I reached the log, I stopped and almost crept to the spot of my dream encounter with the water moccasin. There were the crawdads, still fighting. But nowhere was the snake.

Losing no more time, I continued my journey, reaching Aunt Belle's cabin almost out of breath. Stumbling with exhaustion, I fell into the cabin.

"Dear me, child, what's ailing you?" Aunt Belle stood smiling at me with a large wooden spoon in her hand. There was oatmeal steaming in the pot on the stove and hot biscuits on the table. Two places were set. My gaze went back to Aunt Belle—Aunt Belle in the green dress with the brown circles going around. My eyes grew large.

"My goodness, child, I've been expecting you for days. It gets so lonely here. I'm so glad you've finally come. We'll have breakfast, then work on your quilt. Oh, and I've got some delightful stories to tell you." Aunt Belle turned and began stirring the oatmeal. She was so small, her body nearly bent over. She had always been there when I needed her; now, she needed me.

I walked over and put my arm around her. I was as tall as she. "Aunt Belle, I love you," I said and squeezed her close.

"I love you, too, child." Her eyes were glistening as she kissed my cheek.

As I started to turn, I stopped, surprise holding me rigid. My gaze had traveled to the floor beside the stove, to the puddle of water . . . with the sand in it. Then, shaking my head, I turned to Aunt Belle and said, "Aunt Belle, tell me about the time you met Uncle James. I can't remember how it goes."

"Why, child, I've told you that story a million times. You really like it? Those were the good old days when people knew everyone else in these parts. James was such a dashing young man, and so good-looking! He came to see me in a horse and buggy . . . ."

Aunt Belle was right. I had heard this story scores of times, but I had never noticed the smile on her face, nor the shine in her eyes as she remembered and talked, on and on.

I picked up a biscuit, took a bite of wisdom, and smiled.

Chester and Hector

One of my evening chores was slopping the hogs. Every day all the table scraps were saved and dumped into a galvanized gallon bucket and by evening the bucket was full to overflowing. It took all my strength to lift and carry the heavy load.

The path down to the hog pen curved around the vegetable garden. In the warm night air of late summer, I would trudge through the smell of ripened melons to be hit in the face with the strong odor of the hog pen as I rounded the bend. Walking into the blaze of the setting sun, it smelled as if I were heading into a garden of spoiled cabbage and stagnant pond water! Just beyond, in the shadow of the mountain, was my destination. I could hear the sucking sound of the mud as the hogs' short, sturdy legs sloshed up and down in the mire.

When the hogs finally saw me coming, their floppy ears would start bobbing and slapping in the rush of their mud-sluggish run. My eardrums would hurt with the shrillness of their squeals. What a welcome!

As I drew closer I would start calling, "Hey, Chester! Hey, Hector! Y'all hungry?" The squeals would change to grunts.

Daddy had made a spout through the fence to make it easier for me to dump the slop into the hog trough. For a moment I would stand by the spout, just gazing at the sparkle in the eyes of the hogs as they looked back at me in anticipation, their pink snouts pressed against the wooden slats. I loved those hogs! They needed me; they made me feel their need. It gave me pleasure to dump the slop into the trough.

As they greedily slurped, they allowed me to reach through the slats and rub their heads. I'll never forget the feel of their rough, scaly skin through the stubble of prickly hair, or their satisfied grunts as they would linger for a time, letting me touch them.

Soon, above the now darkened mountaintops, the moon and the stars would join the hogs and me, along with the pulsating calls of the night frogs. It was a pleasurable time there by the hog pen. To some children slopping the hogs was just an unpleasant chore, but to me it was an evening spent with friends.

The Story of the Basket

Aunt Irene used a pocket knife to cut the strips of green wood. After she had the required number of strips, she placed them in a large tub of water to soak. She whittled the ribs for her basket out of heavier strips, long enough to reach around half the basket, making them pointed on both ends. Next, she constructed the handle and bottom rib by looping one long piece of heavy green wood, fastening one inside the other with a nail. Then she began weaving the strips in and out, inserting the ribs by forcing the ends into the weaving as she went.

"Aunt Irene, what kind of wood is that?" I asked. "It splits so good."

"This is white oak, Amy. An' you're right. That's why they're called *splits*. I had your uncle cut the white oak down jest this mornin'. It needs to be split soon as it's cut, sometime in late summer or fall." Her hands moved slowly, yet with knowing sureness.

"Aunt Irene, who taught you how to make a basket?" I asked.

"Reckon it was my mother," she answered.

"And who taught her?"

"Her mother."

"Then it must have been her mother who taught her!" I smiled; I had caught on to this right away.

"Yes, it was. But that's where it ends, though.

Let's see. My mother—your grandma—Ellie Owen, taught me. Her mother, your Great-grandma Sarah Galloway, taught Mama. An' Connie Dawson—your great-great-grandma—taught Grandma Sarah. The real story of the basket, though, came with Grandma Connie, for this basket came into our family with her." She had paused in her work to stare off into space.

"Will you tell me the story?" I leaned forward, sitting as close to her as possible so as not to miss a word. Aunt Irene's eyes twinkled as she saw my interest. When she started to speak, her hands began to weave.

Way back yonder a long time ago, your Grandma Connie came into the mountains with your grandpa and settled on the Tennessee side of the Smokies. When the Civil War started, your grandpa left to fight, leavin' Grandma Connie with their three little girls. 'Tweren't long that your grandma got word that your grandpa was dyin' in one of them war prisons. When Grandma Connie got to him, he was already dead. Grandma couldn't stand it there in Tennessee where she'd spent her time with your grandpa, so's she packed up ever'thang she owned an' set off, her an' them young-uns, in a wagon. She crossed over the mountain into North Carolina and settled on John's Creek.

Your Grandma Connie was a mighty fine woman. She began makin' her livin' by plowin' the fields for her neighbors. I'm told she shore was a strikin' figure with her gold-red hair an' her long dress, callin' to her mules as she furrowed the garden patches for her neighbors.

In the evenin' hours, sittin' by the fireplace, she'd

run her spinnin' wheel, a-spinnin' out yarn for her knittin'. She was known for her love of bright colors for her shawls, a-wrappin' her own self up in a rainbow of color.

Well sir, one fall mornin'—you know—one of them fall mornin's when the leaves are so powerful red they look like splashes of blood, an' the goldenrod is so yeller it looks like the sun's tiptoed all over the pasture, your grandma gets visitors on John's Creek. Up over the mountain nearest to where her spring bubbled up out of the bank, right out of them bright colors, walks a whole band of Cherokee Indians.

I'm not too certain as to Grandma Connie's first thought, but she was smart enough to wait for them to speak first. The Indians moved close to one another, silently, heads high with Cherokee pride. When they saw the woman with the gold-red hair and the shawl of many colors, they stopped an' stared. Then from within their midst came an Indian maiden carrying a wide basket covered with a woven lid. She walked up to Grandma Connie and smiled, extendin' her hand to gently touch the colorful shawl.

One of the braves began to speak, gesturin' toward the spring. Grandma Connie nodded an' the Cherokees moved off to the spring. Then, as the two women smiled at each other, from within the basket held between them came the cry of a baby. They said that the only thing Grandma Connie loved more than bright colors was young-uns. An' shore enough, before long she had the basket opened an' was holdin' that Indian baby. It cooed an' smiled back at her while the Indian mother watched.

The story goes on that the Indian mother shore loved that shawl Grandma Connie had on; she kept touchin' it an' tryin' to talk to Grandma Connie 'bout it. Finally, Grandma Connie just took the shawl off an' wrapped it 'round the young mother's shoulders. Reckon that jest 'bout thrilled the Indian woman to death!

The Cherokees spent the night there close to the spring. Grandma Connie tried to get them to come into the house, but they signed that they simply wanted to stay by the water. She did get the Indian mother to come in for awhile.

In the mornin' when Grandma Connie woke up, she looked out her window toward the spring an' seen that the Indians was fixin' on leavin'. She rushed to dress, an' hurryin' to the door, she flung it open. There on her doorstep stood the Cherokee woman holdin' her child wrapped in the shawl of many colors. An' at Grandma Connie's feet was the basket. The Indian mother motioned to Grandma Connie to take the basket, an' when she did, the mother smiled an' waved goodbye to her new friend.

Grandma Connie shore thought a heap of that first basket. She jest about wore it out usin' it for ever so many things: gatherin' eggs, harvestin' her vegetables, fetchin' wood, an' when it got so's she had jest 'bout wore it out, she kept it close to her holdin' her yarn for her knittin'.

She set her hand at makin' baskets, too, a-studyin' her first one until she got it right. Then she taught her daughter Sarah to make the basket, tellin' her never to forget the friendship of our neighbors, the Cherokee.

An' so, down through the years, the makin' of the basket has been taught from one generation to the next. This basket I'm makin' now is like that same basket given to Grandma Connie.

The room grew quiet. The weaving of the basket continued with skilled hard-working fingers. I gazed thoughtfully at the gold-red hair of the bent head.

"Aunt Irene," I asked, breaking the silence, "will you teach me?"

The Chicken Hawk's Shadow

Of the three of us children, David had the most compassion for animals. Sometimes this put him at odds with our father, who was a hunter and a crack shot with a rifle. But most of the time, the two of them avoided that issue. Instead, Daddy simply gave David the chore of tending to the domestic animals around the house. All he had to do to get the best results from David was to "give" him the animals.

David loved his chickens beyond anything that had ever been given to him. He watched over them with the eye of one whose love knew no limits. The time he spent with them sometimes seemed to be too much for a boy of seven.

Each of the hens had been named carefully, and David recognized each one, calling them by name and knowing simply by sight which hen had laid which egg. He had named his favorite hen Mabel. She had beautiful white fluffy feathers, a rose-colored comb, and sharp, steely eyes. In the summer, she usually had a brood of biddies following her everywhere, causing her white feathers to stay ruffled like one gigantic piece of popcorn.

His one rooster's name was Dominique, mainly because most of his chickens were of the breed known as Dominickers. Dominique was a magnificent specimen of male power! He carried his black and white feathers around like a cape over the shoulders of a lord, strutting about our dirt yard as if it were the jeweled courtyard of a castle.

One summer was really a scorcher! The creek had dwindled down to just a stream, the tall bank grass at the foot of the mountains had turned to field straw, and the snakes and lizards had come to call in the chicken coop many a night. Since the chickens had the run of our little cove, they had taken to roosting in trees nearby and laying their eggs in the bushes on the banks of the mountains.

At periodic times every day that summer, a high-pitched alarm would suddenly erupt from the throat of Dominique. His proud plumage would seem to collapse, drawing close to his body, as his neck would stretch way beyond its normal length. At the sound of Dominique's alarm, all the hens and biddies would scurry away, finding the closest cover. Only after all were hidden would Dominique run for cover.

Moments later, a flying shadow with long pointed wings would suddenly drape its image over the yard. Above us, in the sky, the flying chicken hawk didn't look so ominous; it was his shadow that carried fear. For there was no doubt that the shadow carried malice or even death as it circled.

To the three of us children, it seemed at these times that the world would grow as still as an icicle, with sounds coming in drop-whispers. The only thing that would move would be Doris, for sometimes she would drop to the ground and trace the image of the shadow of the chicken hawk in the dirt. David would almost always explode in a flurry of dust as he would stomp out the drawing. Then, we'd all laugh and the tension would be broken.

After awhile, the chicken hawk would fly away and the chickens would once again come out to scratch around in the dirt of the yard. Everything would be back to normal. But one day something happened that shattered the normal.

The hot morning sun had just come torching over the east mountain. David was feeding the chickens. Throwing shelled corn out all about him, he had called them out from the scrubs with a loud "Here chick! Here chick! Here chick, chick, chic-c-ck!" Dust flew from the parched ground as the chickens rushed to the easy pickings. Even Mabel had herded her young ones out to try the corn.

After tossing out all the feed to the group, David found this a perfect time to hold "school." He set his bucket down and began to talk to the chickens as if they were students in a class on tidiness.

"Dominique," he began, getting right in the rooster's face, "you an' them hens gotta stay off the porch. Mother don't like you all leaving your droppings where she walks. She's threatening to have one of you chickens for Sunday dinner. You hear me?"

He turned to Mabel. "Mabel, you an' them biddies got into Daddy's tomatoes out there in the garden. He ain't partial to putting out his hard work jest to have it pecked up by you chickens. Ain't no tellin' what's gonna happen to you if he gets a-holt of you!"

From where I sat dangling my feet off the porch, I began to laugh at the seriousness of David's conversation with the chickens who actually seemed to be listening to him.

Suddenly, without any warning, swift powerful wings drawn high in a plunge slipped almost noiselessly down beside David into the group of chickens, and a long slim brown body pounced with lightning speed onto one of Mabel's biddies. The chicken hawk's sharp curved talons dug into the chirping chick with a vise-like grip and then the hawk flew away.

Stricken, David cried out with a strangled, almost unearthly sound. His face white, tears swelled into his eyes and refused to roll. They just seemed to hang there, glistening in anguish.

There had been no warning shadow, for the sun had not climbed high enough in the sky. There had been no warning from Dominique. The early morning swiftness of the hawk had prohibited his detection. David's tears dried as he shook his head in immediate anger. His small hands balled into fists; his toes curved into his bare feet as if the ground had become too hot to stand on. A look of determination began to grow, even before he cried out. "Daddy! Daddy!" his voice echoed in the early morning.

I jumped down and ran to stand behind my brother, feeling an urgent need to comfort him. The back door opened and Daddy appeared with a dipper in his hand.

"What's goin' on?" he asked.

"Daddy, that chicken hawk got one of Mabel's chicks!" David stalked toward Daddy.

"Well, it had to happen sometime, Son. There ain't much for them to eat out there in this kind of weather." Daddy drank out of the dipper and then wiped his mouth with the back of his hand.

"Daddy," David said as he stopped before him, "I want you to learn me how to shoot a gun!"

Daddy stared at the angry boy. "Well now, . . . you

thinkin' on shootin' or killin' yourself a chicken hawk?"

David drew back a step as he heard the frank words. Then, as his anger began to evaporate in the heavy heat of the day and the moment, he spoke in a more measured voice, "I reckon I need to help Dominique take care of his family. Maybe I can scare the hawk so's he won't come back."

"Good enough reason, I 'spect. We'll take a go at the rifle this evenin' after supper. Who knows, maybe you'd like to go squirrel huntin' with me come season. Time you learned how to be a real man, anyway!" As Daddy turned to go back inside the kitchen, David whirled back toward me. Daddy never saw the sick look that had quickly descended upon David's face.

"You ain't hankerin' to kill anything, are you, David?" My voice cut through the dust our bare feet stirred up as we walked over to where we could hear Mabel clucking close to the creek.

David stopped, and looked me square in the eyes. "Amy, I ain't never gonna kill a livin' thang as long as I live myself . . . not even a chicken hawk. Ain't nobody gonna make me!" He swallowed and lowered his eyes for a moment and when he looked up he had tears in his eyes. "Ain't I real already? I don't have to kill a little animal to be a real man, do I?"

David learned how to shoot a rifle, and even a shotgun. As he practiced with Daddy at the old oak out back, I watched the gun slap against his shoulder, knocking him down over and over again. Soon the shadow of the chicken hawk was almost a thing of the past, for David practiced his scare tactics with the rifle often.

Come season, David went squirrel hunting with

Daddy. But, it was no time at all that Daddy quit taking him. After that, I remember Daddy always saying that David "shore had no eye for shootin' . . . couldn't hit the broad side of a barn!"

As for me, I think different.

Granny's Rows of Jars

My Granny beat all! I've never seen anyone like her. When she was ninety-eight years old she was living by herself, still tending her own garden. She wore dresses with the hem down to her high-top shoes, a bonnet to shade her eyes, and always, she wore a white apron over her dress. She outlived Grandpa and every one of her young-uns except one.

Granny was just a girl when she and Grandpa got married. It was sometime just before the War Between the States. Grandpa and Grandma built a cabin back in a hollow up on Wolf Mountain and began raising a family. Grandpa was a preacher and he preached at nearly every revival in the mountains. He didn't hold with killing, so Granny didn't lose her man to the mighty war, she lost him to his circuit riding.

Until their young-uns grew big enough to help, Granny worked the farm herself. She milked the cows, she slopped the hogs, she made all her children's clothes. She plowed, planted, and took care of the garden. She had a root cellar where she stored all the jars of vegetables she put away. That root cellar was stocked. When you went in with a lamp held high, there were rows of jars shining at you. The neighbors around and about all soon got to know she was a woman not to be reckoned with when it came to hard work and conserving. Granny certainly was a conserving soul! She was always putting something away for a rainy day.

On my sixth birthday, I had walked over to Granny's because I knew she'd have something for me. Granny saw me coming, so she left her hoe laying among the corn rows and met me in front of the porch. On the porch sat Calico, Granny's cat.

"I got something for your birthday, Amy," she said. "You wait right here whilst I fetch it."

Well, just like all little girls, I wanted to pet that cat, but Calico didn't hold with petting. I reckoned I'd get a hold on him anyway, so I chased him around and around the porch until he had enough and jumped through an open window. Looking to follow him, I pulled back the curtains and started to climb inside. But, all at once, the sunlight bounced against something in the room and then smack dab into my eyes. I blinked. I could hardly believe what I saw!

There was Granny with her back to me, facing a cabinet with its doors standing open. As I looked through the window, I saw rows and rows of jars lining the shelves of the cabinet. My heart began jumping up and down, because even though I was just a child, I knew the glint of money. I had never seen the likes of such wealth before. Some of the jars were full of coins and some were filled with green paper. Granny didn't see me. She stepped back to close the cabinet, and I started to run. Scared and excited all at the same time, I headed back to the front of the house.

"Here you go, honey," said Granny as she came out the door. "Here's a penny for every year you've grown. Six coppers the color of your hair!"

I ran all the way home. Whispering loud and rolling my eyes, I told Mother about Granny's jars of money. "Granny's r-rich!" I stuttered. "I ain't never seen so much m-money. She ga-gave me some!"

Mother stared at me for a minute. "You told Granny thank you, didn't you?" she asked.

I hung my head.

Seeing my shame, Mother patted my arm. "Don't take on now, Amy, you were a mite excited. Granny's saved all her life. Everything she's ever reaped, she's put away in glass jars so she can see the fruit of her labor. She just wants to look at it; she can't bear to part with it. You have to remember, Amy, none of what you saw is yours, so you best forget you ever saw it. What's Granny's is Granny's. She'll take care of her own. You do the same."

What Mother told me I didn't understand until I grew older. Her words came back to haunt me when I did what I did. It was all because of the mystery that came out of Granny's glass jars of money. You see, years later, when she died, the family went looking for those jars. But they were gone! All of them . . . gone!

I was ten years old then, and I felt *I* knew right where to look. I knew the jars were there because I had seen them myself. I sneaked back out there one night all by myself. It was a night when everybody had

gone to prayer meeting and I begged off because of a "bellyache."

The moon was like an owl's eye, shining bright; I could see everything clearly. I swung the hoe high, digging where I had seen Granny digging a time before she died, in her flower bed near the porch. It was no time until I heard the sound of my hoe hitting glass.

My own heartbeat suddenly thumped in my ears. And then there began a real funny feeling in my backbone, like somebody was watching me. I looked over my shoulder. There was nothing. I looked up toward the old vacant house. Seemed I could almost see Granny in her white apron standing there on the porch, telling me her coppers were the color of my hair. Those same hairs stood up on the back of my neck! I made the dirt fly!

There it was! I saw the sparkle of glass in the moonlight. I hooked my hoe onto the lid of the jar and taking a deep breath, I used all the strength I had and gave a jerk, dropping the hoe as the ground suddenly let go! Dirt flew in my face as the jar almost jumped into my hands. Spitting and sputtering, I wasted no time twisting off that lid.

Sure enough, it was one of Granny's jars. I knew it right away, because, with a sickness in my belly, I knew what I was looking at in that jar was the bones of Calico, the cat.

Disappointment almost overcame me as I leaned back against the porch. All at once, something brushed my back. I didn't wait for anything else; I flung that jar back over my shoulder and left the flower bed running. I never looked back.

Granny's house is gone now, but the old chimney stands. The money was never found. But every time some of the family goes to visit the old place, seems there's some new dirt been turned up, as if somebody's been digging. And every once in a while, they tell me they've found a crusted-over coin or two.

Me, . . . well, I don't go anywhere near!

Velvet and the Missionary Box

In the winter it takes the sun longer to climb over the mountains, so, in this blustery season, daybreak comes late. In those dark mornings, when the rooster crowed the first time, he sounded far away, but when he crowed the second time and flapped his wings, I knew Mother would soon be telling my sister, brother, and me to "rise and shine!" When we arose from our mattress made of cornhusks, it was still dark outside—really dark! The darkness soon gave way to the beginning of a bright day in the high land of the Blue Ridge.

Getting dressed for school in the winter had to be done as quickly as possible. There was no heat in the bedroom, and no light. Kerosene lamps in the front room cast our shadows on the walls as we ran over cold linoleum floors to crowd around the pot-bellied stove. Here we finished dressing. The red-hot stove heated first one side of our bodies, then the other.

Our clothes, fashioned from the cotton or broadcloth material of feed sacks or flour sacks, were all made by our mother, and each of us had only one pair of shoes. But once in a while Daddy would buy a box of used clothing from a missionary at Tuckasegee, and Mother would remake the clothes to fit us. It was then we thought we were rich!

On our way to school one morning, Doris and I were discussing how pretty we were in our new dresses.

Trudging alongside us, David listened to our every word. Three years younger than I, he was at that wonderful stage of youth when he believed everything I said. He pressed close while I explained to Doris that we were probably the best-dressed kids at Tuckasegee Elementary School, not only because Mother had made these dresses, but because the whole box from the missionary had cost Daddy only three dollars and we would soon have many more dresses made out of the treasures of that same box.

That afternoon my sister invited her best friend Wilma Milsaps to spend the night with us. Wilma's father was an important business man, a tobacco farmer, in Tuckasegee. The clothes Wilma wore were all "store bought."

That night we were sitting in the front room, just talking. During the conversation, Wilma began to compliment Doris on her dress. "Such a beautiful dress, Doris," she said. "I love the color! And it fits you so good. You look like a model in the catalog down at Doc Moses' store."

Doris smiled happily at Wilma. "I love it, too," she said. "It feels so good next to my skin."

"That's because it's velvet," responded Wilma. "I don't have one like that. I've been asking Mom to get me one. You're so lucky! I wish I had a dress like yours!"

David had been lying on the floor, coloring in a coloring book, listening, of course, as all little brothers do. At that last statement of Wilma's, he jumped up and ran over to the two girls.

"Wilma," he told her excitedly, "I know how you can have a dress just like that! Tell your daddy to go over to Mrs. Farmer's house—you know, the missionary by the church—and get one of them boxes of clothes! They only cost three dollars! Your mom can make you one."

There grew a total silence in the room. It seemed to last an eternity.

It's a true wonder David survived. If looks could kill, he would have died a slow death right there with the look Doris turned on him! Wilma handled it as a good friend should have, though. Leaning toward Doris, she simply ran her hand over the velvet, and changed the subject.

The little guy had meant well, although he had embarrassed both his sisters. We finally did forgive him, because we three "stuck together." At that point, our lives were just beginning to change. Trouble was on the horizon for us, and we truly would need each other's support in the days to come.

A Shoe-Box Christmas

From our front yard we could see only tall mountains covered with towering pines, stretching toward the sky, closing us in a world all our own. We seemed to be all alone, and time, for a while, stood still.

It had been almost a year since our move to Tuckasegee. At first, life had been almost scary, but the newness had slowly developed into solid ways of caring for one another. As the year went on, however, a more serious situation had developed. Daddy had found little work, and Mother had first become ill, then bedridden. Her auburn hair spread out on her pillow, framing the paleness of her face.

Mother's illness had left its mark on all of us, but it had affected David the most. His world had revolved around our mother, but now she paid him little attention. Confused, he had begun seeking me out.

Doris, our chatterbox, had grown very quiet. Her gaze often strayed toward the back room in which Mother had confined herself. And sometimes, in the night, lying next to my sister, I could hear her crying. I felt the weight of the lonely dark house on my chest.

Our only source of entertainment was the battery-operated radio. In the evenings the world of imagination took over as we listened to "The Lone Ranger," "The Shadow," "Gunsmoke," and "The Cisco Kid." David, engrossed in the westerns, wore an old felt hat of Daddy's, the brim resting on his ears, and carried a stick in his overalls which, he declared, had to be the fastest gun in the West!

That year David wanted Santa to bring him his own cowboy hat and a set of low-hanging play guns. Doris shyly suggested she would like to have an honest-to-goodness pad of drawing paper and a box of crayons. She was tired of drawing birds in the sand on the road; she wanted to put the color of the sky into her bluebirds. I decided it was my job, as the oldest, to bring the spirit of Christmas into this sad home.

The night before I had heard on the radio that we were going to have snow for Christmas. That in itself was exciting, for we all loved snow! So I told my little brother he should start praying for snow, that Santa could not drive his sleigh if there were no snow. (Of course, I expected to see the white stuff drifting down around us at any minute.) Then I told Doris and David that the elves were working extra long hours at the North Pole, making gifts especially for them. Guessing games began between the two as to who was going to get what.

A wonderful idea came to me! We could climb the mountain behind the house and cut the Christmas tree. I had helped Daddy chop down the tree year after year, and I was big enough now to handle it myself, I was sure. We could get the tree and surprise Daddy when he returned from Grandpa's house later that day.

I jumped up, calling, "Doris! David! Get your coats! We're going to go get the Christmas tree!"

Happiness flooded their faces as they ran to do my bidding. "Hooray! Christmas is coming!" They almost sang in their attempt to hurry.

I went to the bedroom to tell Mother that we were going out for awhile. She was asleep, so I tiptoed out of the bedroom, motioning to David and Doris to be quiet. Donning our coats, the three of us quietly left the house, closing the door behind us. I ran to the smokehouse to get Daddy's small hatchet, and then up we climbed, checking the trees as we went.

"Amy, look! Here's one . . . naw, the back's out."

"This one! This one . . . nope, guess not. It's crooked!" We were getting close to the fence row when we saw the perfect one. It was a balsam, just about as tall as I was. A cold wind began to blow as I started to chop. Out of the corner of my eye, I could see my brother and sister shivering. But, in spite of the cold, smiles covered their faces. The weather didn't seem to matter.

Doris and David carried the tree down the glade, one on either side of the trunk. As we went down the hill, we began singing, "Here comes Santa Claus, here comes Santa Claus, right down Santa Claus lane. . . ."

Upon reaching the house, I went back to the smokehouse to put away the hatchet, and there I found a pail.

"David, you and Doris see if you can find some dirt that's not frozen to put around the trunk," I called over my shoulder as I set the tree down into the pail. They went scurrying off as I picked up the tree and the pail and carried them into the house. The warmth of the wood stove greeted me as I came into the living room. The sweet smell of balsam brought Christmas closer. Doris and David came in lugging a bucket of dirt.

"David, run down to the spring and get some water to give the tree a drink." I laughed as I swept up the floor. As he hurried out, I could feel Doris's eyes on me. "Amy, what are we going to do for decorations?" she asked. Leaning on the broom handle, I tried to think fast.

"How about stringing some popcorn?" she suddenly suggested brightly.

"Great!" I said, picking up her excitement. "That's just what we'll do. And then we can stir up some paste—you know, out of flour and water—and cut up that colored paper we got from school and make chains."

As Doris hurried into the kitchen to look for the popcorn, David came in, hunched over with the weight of the water he carried. "Thanks, David. Maybe you can think of something to make our tree pretty. Doris is popping corn and I'm going to make some colored paper chains."

David helped me dip the water around the tree trunk, pondering all the while. Then as I straightened, my gaze fell on his face just as his idea struck.

"I know just what to get!" he cried and dashed through the door. In his haste, he let the door slam.

"Amy! Amy! What's going on?" Mother called from the bedroom. I hurried over to the bedroom door, stopping just inside the doorway, adjusting my eyes to the darkened room. Mother was trying to sit up.

"It's okay, Mother. Just David running out! He's all excited about our Christmas tree. We chopped it ourselves! It's going to be so-o-o pretty! Just wait, you'll see!"

Mother's eyes filled with tears as she beckoned to me. "Amy, I'm praying that I get better soon," she

began, reaching for my hands. I could feel her tremble. "But I'm afraid Christmas will be very small this year," she continued, "very small, and sad."

Her cheeks were wet as she talked. My throat grew tight. I hugged her close, and when I could speak, I whispered, "That's okay, Mother, that's okay."

She lay back on the pillow and closed her eyes. I stood up and straightened the covers on her bed, pulling them up over her arms. I could feel the coldness of the room drying my face.

"Mother, are you hungry? Want something to eat? I made some corn bread and tomato stew awhile ago."

She opened her eyes and looked at me with a new expression. "Yes," she said, "I think . . . I will have some. Just a bit, though." Eagerly, I ran out to heat the stew. It was the first time she'd been interested in eating in many days.

As I stood with Doris at the stove, the smell of stew and popcorn filling the room, David ran in with his eyes shining, hiding something behind his back. "Look!" he cried. "Look what I have!" Slowly, he brought his arm around to show us an old bird's nest with a blue egg nestled in the middle. "It didn't hatch, so I think the mama bird left her pretty blue egg for our tree."

Doris clapped her hands and bent over David's treasure. "It's so pretty, David," she said. "Our tree's going to be something special. Maybe I can even draw it!"

As the three of us stood in the warm kitchen, I felt the most complete feeling of wonderful discovery. We were creating our own Christmas spirit.

That evening we strung popcorn, made flour paste, and glued our chains. Then we decorated the tree with the chains draped all around the branches, intermingled with strings of popcorn. And, near the top, we placed David's bird's nest.

Mother had been able to get up after eating the stewed tomatoes and was sitting in Daddy's big chair, covered with a patchwork quilt. She smiled often and enjoyed our clowning and singing.

It was after dark when we heard Daddy's footsteps on the floorboards of the porch. "Ho!" he laughed, "what's this ruckus? Could hear you half way up the mountain!"

Daddy came in and had his coat almost off when he saw our tree. For a second, I thought I could see sadness in his eyes, but then he smiled and said, "Ah, you've got the tree all done. And it's a fine job indeed! Come and give your Pop a hug!"

What a fine time we had that night.

The next day was Christmas Eve. As soon as my eyes opened, I bounced out of bed and ran to the window. There had to be snow, but there wasn't. I was so disappointed. Then immediately, I began to try to think of something to tell David, just in case it really didn't snow for Christmas.

As I built a fire in the wood stove in the living room, I thought of all kinds of things. Maybe Santa was teaching the reindeer to pull the sleigh without snow. Or maybe Rudolph had a cold and couldn't come if it was snowing!

"Amy! There ain't no snow!"

David, in his flannel nightshirt, stood barefoot in the

doorway to the bedroom, unhappiness written all over his face.

I had to think fast! Quickly, I swept him close in my arms, saying, "We've got a whole day yet, David. Let's bake a cake for Christmas, want to?"

"Oh, boy! Cake! I'll crack some walnuts, okay?" The disappointment was gone from his face.

We spent Christmas Eve baking and sneaking around the house making little presents for each other. Christmas cards for Mother and Daddy were drawn and shaded in with charcoal. To us they were masterpieces.

I noticed Mother and Daddy in the bedroom talking quite a bit. Daddy sat on the edge of Mother's bed, but their voices were too low for me to hear what was said. I knew it wasn't happy news, for when Daddy left for town about midday, his face was full of sadness. Afterwards I could hear Mother crying softly.

In order to keep David and Doris laughing while we were baking, I took cocoa and sugar, mixed them, and put the mixture under my tongue. I pretended that it was snuff like Grandma's. Getting an old tin can, as she did, I would talk and then spit, talk and spit. Doris and David thought that was hilarious!

Then, out of the oven came our creation, decorating the house with the warm smell of sweetness. We made the icing by beating an egg white, then piled the cake high with peaks of white, while David covered it all with walnut pieces. It was beautiful!

Afterwards, toward evening, we all sat down around the stove in the living room and talked. I told Doris and David the story of the Christ Child as I had been told many times over, and how the wise men had

brought the newborn baby gifts because they loved him. Their eyes glowed in the dim light of the kerosene lamp.

Some time later, I got up to check on Mother, and coming back into the living room, I passed the window and looked out. There was Daddy walking down the path from the road above the house. He was carrying a brown paper sack. His hat was pulled down over his face. He went into the smokehouse and came out without the bag.

"Hello, kids! How's your mother this evening?" Daddy hung his coat on a nail by the door and sat in his chair by the stove, leaning forward, rubbing his hands together.

"She's asleep, Daddy. But she ate good a while ago."

"Well, that's good! Maybe she's getting better. Let's hope so. Say! What did you kids do today?"

Doris and David ran to either side of him and talked at the same time. As I stood by the window, I looked out again, hoping to see snow coming down in the twilight. But, as before, there was none.

David was suddenly tugging at my sleeve. He had found Daddy's old hat and was wearing it pushed back on top of his head.

"Amy, let's get to bed! Maybe Santa will really bring me some guns if he sees my hat!"

"Now, David, you can't sleep in your hat!"

Lying in bed later, I could hear the low murmur of Mother and Daddy talking together. Once again I could sense a feeling of sadness in their low conversation.

"Please God," I prayed, "let Santa come for my sister

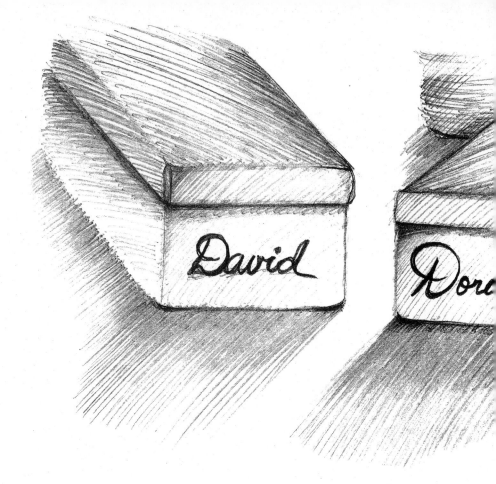

and brother!" I prayed with my hands clasped, and with all my being. "And, please God, let Mom get well soon, real soon."

Just before going to sleep I remember thinking I could hear jingle bells.

I awoke to a still dark room on Christmas morning. Doris and David were still sleeping. Quietly, I slipped off the bed and tiptoed out of the bedroom and over to the Christmas tree. There under the tree were three shoe boxes, each one marked with one of our names.

I sat down on the cold wooden floor and put my box in my lap. It was not gift wrapped and had no ribbon. Slowly, I opened the box. Inside was an orange, an apple, a small bag of peppermint candy, and the rest of

the box was filled with a mixture of nuts.

As I sat there, I knew that for us, Santa was our Dad, trudging to town on foot, with hardly any money, and coming back with something—all he and Mother could afford—for their children. In my mind, I could see Daddy again as he came down the trail with his brown paper bag.

Getting up from the floor, I walked to the window to see our Christmas morning. I gasped with happiness at the winter wonderland outside the cabin, for snow covered everything!

Blinking away the tears in my eyes, I turned back to the cold room, and looked again at my shoe box—my shoe box full of diamonds and jewels.

The Ever After

Those years in the Tuckasegee Valley were wonderful years for us, the Ammons kids. We three learned to face the world side by side, every day, because we had to. Beyond the horizon was a mystery, something to dream about.

The memory of us walking together down the mountain on school mornings is caught in my mind like the mist that always rises just before dawn. We'd stay close together. The sun would slyly edge over the tall trees, and to us the weeds, bushes, and trees growing near the bank of Grassy Creek Road would sometimes, in the morning darkness, become images of ogres, giants, wildcats, and panthers.

But soon the red glow of the sun would fully emerge to light our way. It was then that we'd begin to observe the wonders of nature all around us: the sparkle of the frozen icicles hanging from some of the high banks of dirt alongside the road, the dancing diamond-like sparks of mica flakes in our pathway, and the glowing dew caught and held by the silken strands of a spider web spanning a laurel bush.

Sometimes, instead of walking down the road, we'd take a shortcut through the woods. We had worn our own trail in the rugged terrain, and there was a spot about halfway down where we would stop and look at the deep valley. The mist would be gone, dissolved by the bright rays of the sun.

The Tuckasēgee River would look like part of a bright silver necklace as it wound its way west; the sky would reflect the bluest of blue from the many spirals of smoke rising from the chimneys of our neighbors; and the smell of burning wood would float in the breeze as we continued on our way. At last, to our despair, we could also see the yellow of our bus as it moved its way along Route 107 toward us.

This halfway point is where we would have liked to have remained forever—caught between home and school. We were innocent; we were full of dreams; we were together.

Doris, David, and I grew to be very close during those mornings of early childhood, so close that even now we know a special bond which developed from depending on one another for support and from sharing dreams. Now, when we are together at my brother's cabin on Grassy Creek Road, we walk the same dirt, mica-flaked road we walked as children and find that we are still caught and held with the mist in a silken web of memories.

And when we travel through Tuckasegee, our heads turn, almost at the same time, toward the old house where the missionary used to live. Then we look at each other and smile, for we still wear velvet—it's in our eyes.

Amy Ammons Garza, Author and Storyteller

Several years after leaving the Tuckasegee Valley, Amy began studying creative writing at Purdue University Calumet (Indiana) with Professor Charles Tinkham. Winner of over thirty awards for short stories, personal essays, children's literature, poetry, and novels, she is currently associate editor for "Transport Fleet News," a trucking magazine in Chicago.

Amy's first book, *Retter, A Novel of the Mountains* is based on her grandmother's life. Her second novel, *Cannie, the Hills of Home*, is the story of her mother. Book three in the series of mountain women stories, gleaned from her heritage in the North Carolina mountains, is in progress.

Together with her sister Doreyl, Amy founded Catch the Spirit of Appalachia, a nonprofit organization based in Tuckasegee dedicated to promoting literacy and awareness of self-worth in both children and adults. They developed a creative process entitled "Opening Doors to Creativity," which is presented in the workbook *Catch the Spirit of Creativity*, also published by Bright Mountain Books. It contains creative exercises used successfully in their workshops as visiting artists in public school systems in California, Indiana, Illinois, and North and South Carolina.

Doreyl Ammons, Artist and Workshop Leader

Doris Ammons and Doreyl Ammons are one and the same. Returning to North Carolina in 1992, Doris combined her given names, Doris Ellen, into Doreyl. With a masters degree in bio-medical art and science, Doreyl has spent over twenty years in the commercial art and advertising field as president and owner of an advertising agency in southern California. An experienced workshop leader, Doreyl brings a commitment to creating an environment in which participants can experience their unique creativity. She has exhibited in group and individual shows in California, Indiana, and Washington, D.C.

Although she has illustrated the covers of her sister's books, *Matchbox Mountain* is Doreyl's book-illustration debut.